Aliens
Don't Wear
Braces

There are more books about the Bailey School Kids!
Have you read these adventures?

Vampires Don't Wear Polka Dots
Santa Claus Doesn't Mop Floors
Leprechauns Don't Play Basketball
Werewolves Don't Go to Summer Camp
Ghosts Don't Eat Potato Chips
Frankenstein Doesn't Plant Petunias

Aliens Don't Wear Braces

by **Debbie Dadey**
and
Marcia Thornton Jones

illustrated by John Steven Gurney

A
LITTLE APPLE
PAPERBACK

SCHOLASTIC INC.

New York   Toronto   London   Auckland   Sydney

*For the students at Mary Todd, James Lane Allen,
Russell Cave, and Tates Creek Elementary
Schools in Lexington, Kentucky — even those
who wear braces!
— DD and MTJ*

ISBN 0-590-47070-1

12 11 10 9 8 7 6 5 4 3 2   3 4 5 6 7 8/9

Printed in the U.S.A.   28

First Scholastic printing, October 1993

Book design by Laurie McBarnette

1

Power Surge

Howie hung his purple bookbag in his third-grade classroom at Bailey Elementary School. "Did you study for the science test?" he asked his friend Eddie.

Eddie scratched his curly red hair and dropped his bookbag on the floor. "Naw. Who needs science, anyway?"

"I like science," Howie told him. "Especially when it's about outer space."

"You would. You have plenty of empty space between your ears." Eddie laughed and headed for his seat.

The other kids in the class were busy copying math problems from the board. School had not even started and Mrs. Jeepers, their teacher, already had everyone working!

There was something strange about

1

their third-grade teacher. Mrs. Jeepers was from the Transylvanian Alps and some kids thought she was a vampire. Her long hair was the color of a jack-o'-lantern, and a bat bracelet hung from her wrist. She always wore a huge green brooch and when she got mad, it glowed. Mrs. Jeepers had a way of flashing her green eyes that made kids think twice about causing trouble.

Eddie slid into his seat and tore a piece of paper from his notebook. He was only halfway finished copying the math problems when Mrs. Jeepers spoke in her Transylvanian accent. "It is time to take the science test. Please clear off your desks."

Melody's seat was beside Eddie. She twirled one of her black pigtails. "I hope I get a good grade. Don't you?"

Carey was behind Melody. "I studied all weekend. I'm sure I'll get the highest grade."

Eddie shrugged. "Who cares?"

Liza, a girl in front of Eddie, turned to look at him. "You did study, didn't you? After all, this is a big test. I just hope my nose doesn't start bleeding." When Liza was really upset, her nose usually bled.

"I'll give you a bloody nose," Eddie kidded, holding up his fist.

Melody glared at Eddie and handed Liza a wad of tissues. "Leave Liza alone or I'll give you a bloody nose!"

Eddie didn't have time to answer because Mrs. Jeepers put a paper on his desk. "There will be no talking," she told the students. "You may begin."

Eddie looked at the first question. He swallowed hard and looked at the next question. He was searching the second page for something he could answer when he heard a noise.

It sounded like someone was playing a low note on a tuba. The hum grew louder

and louder until the windows rattled. Melody slapped her hands over her ears and Liza whimpered, "What is that?"

Suddenly, all the lights flickered and then went out.

2

Missing Teacher

Mrs. Jeepers' eyes flashed at the ceiling. Then she touched her brooch. The green pin glowed mysteriously. The lights flickered again, and then stayed on. "You may continue with your test," she said quietly, still looking at the ceiling.

Eddie turned around to talk to Howie. "What's going on?"

Howie held his finger to his lips. "Shhh."

But it was too late. Mrs Jeepers walked up to Eddie and scooped up his paper. "Talking during tests is not permitted," she said in her strange accent. "You must speak with Principal Davis."

Eddie's face turned bright red. "But I wasn't cheating."

Mrs. Jeepers touched her green brooch

again and her eyes flashed. Melody gasped and Liza closed her eyes. Would Mrs. Jeepers do something terrible to him? Eddie didn't wait to find out. He slid from his desk and stomped out of the room.

The principal's office was a wreck. The secretary was pushing buttons and yelling into the intercom system for the art teacher while a second-grade teacher was talking with Principal Davis. Twenty-eight second-graders wandered around the office, pulling stuff off the secretary's desk and playing tag with each other.

Eddie plopped into a chair to watch the excitement. A tall woman with long white hair sat next to him. She wore a white shirt with big silver buttons, black leggings, and black boots that came up above her knees. Her face was long and thin and whiter than chalk dust. She smiled at him, showing a mouth full of metal braces.

"You're too old to have braces," Eddie blurted.

The woman shrugged. "What makes you think I am old?"

"You have white hair," Eddie told her.

The tall woman smiled again. "My hair may not be the delightful color of Jupiter like yours, but where I come from some people think I look young. And people are never too old to wear braces." Then she looked at Principal Davis.

"Are you waiting to see the principal?" Eddie asked her. "Because if you are, it might be a while. This place is a zoo."

The tall woman frowned and looked around the room. "There are no animals here," she said.

"I don't mean a real zoo," Eddie started to explain.

"It does not matter," the strange woman interrupted and pulled some papers out of her briefcase. "I will not have to wait much longer."

The second-grade teacher was still talking to Principal Davis.

"But my students are supposed to have art now," she was saying. "Where could the art teacher be?"

Principal Davis shook his head. "Mr. Gibson's car is in the parking lot and I saw him earlier this morning. He must be somewhere. First there was that electrical power surge, and now the art teacher is missing. If only there was a substitute teacher who could teach the art classes!"

The lady winked at Eddie before she walked up to Principal Davis and handed him her papers. "Hello, my name is Mrs. Zork. I am looking for a teaching job."

Principal Davis' mouth dropped open as he looked at Mrs. Zork's papers. "Can you teach art?"

"Art is my specialty," she said. "As a matter of fact, where I come from, my pottery is displayed in the capital."

Principal Davis grinned and gestured to the kids running circles around his desk. "They're all yours, Mrs. Zork."

As soon as the tall woman left with the children, Principal Davis looked at his secretary. "That was lucky."

Eddie watched the tall woman walk down the hall and whispered, "I think it's creepy."

3

Mrs. Zork

When Eddie got back from the principal's office, his class was lining up for art.

"Did you get in trouble?" Howie asked softly.

"Naw. Principal Davis was too busy chasing second-graders," Eddie told him.

"Those flickering lights were weird," Howie whispered to Eddie. "Even Mrs. Jeepers thought so."

"Speaking of weird, you should see the new art teacher," Eddie said.

"New art teacher? What happened to Mr. Gibson?" Liza asked.

Eddie shrugged. "No one knows. Not even Principal Davis."

"You're lying," Melody said. "Teachers don't just disappear."

"They do at Bailey Elementary," Eddie snapped.

"What's strange about this new art teacher?" Howie interrupted.

"For one thing, she looks like she fell into a bag of flour," Eddie told them. "Her face is so white I bet her blood has been sucked dry by Count Dracula."

"Maybe Mrs. Jeepers got her," Melody giggled.

"I think Eddie's exaggerating," Liza told her.

"You'll find out when you see her," Eddie told his friends as they left their classroom.

"I beg your pardon," Mrs. Jeepers said when she opened the art room door. "I am looking for Mr. Gibson."

The tall woman smiled at the class. The kids stared at her white face and silver braces. "I am the substitute, Mrs. Zork."

Mrs. Jeepers flashed her eyes. "But

I am certain I saw Mr. Gibson this morning. He did not say anything about leaving."

"Maybe he's sick," Liza blurted.

Mrs. Zork spoke so softly they had to strain to hear. "Mr Gibson had to leave . . . unexpectedly."

Mrs. Jeepers nodded. "I am sure no one will give Mrs. Zork any trouble." She looked straight at Eddie before she left.

The kids sat down at the paint-stained tables. "I am pleased to visit your school," Mrs. Zork told them. "I look forward to learning much from you."

"Don't you mean that we're going to learn from you?" Carey asked.

"But, of course," Mrs. Zork said softly. "We shall begin by having a pottery lesson."

"But what about the totem poles we were making?" Liza asked.

"Totem poles?" Mrs. Zork asked. "I know nothing about totem poles. But I am quite the expert at throwing clay pots."

Eddie laughed. "I'm good at throwing stuff, too!"

Mrs. Zork flashed her braces at Eddie. "Then you may be the first to demonstrate!" Before Eddie could complain, Mrs. Zork grabbed his hand and plopped a big blob of clay in front of him.

The clay was on a small table. Mrs. Zork pushed a button with her foot and the table began to whirl. Mrs. Zork held Eddie's hands in the clay and together they began forming a pot.

"That's neat," Liza said. "May I try?"

"Certainly." Mrs. Zork let go of Eddie's hands. Eddie quickly slipped away from the table and Liza took his place.

Liza pressed hard on the clay blob as the table whirled around. "I can't get it right," she complained.

"Yours looks like a hamburger," Carey said.

"Looks more like a flying saucer to me," Howie giggled.

"Do you mean an interplanetary transportation system?" Mrs. Zork asked.

Howie nodded. "I know all about spaceships. My dad works at the Federal Aeronautics Technology Station and he has all kinds of books about space."

Mrs. Zork's braces seemed to glow when she smiled at Howie. "That is very interesting information."

"FATS is where all the space nerds work," Eddie muttered, flicking little blobs of clay across the room.

"This is messy," Liza interrupted. Her hands were covered with slimy gray clay.

Melody laughed. "That's because you're all thumbs!"

Mrs Zork's braces sparked as she grabbed Liza's hands. "This child is not all thumbs," she said softly. "Her hands are just as human hands should be."

All the kids laughed.

"Quit laughing at me," Liza stammered.

"Don't get upset," Melody told her friend. "Your nose will start bleeding." But it was too late. Liza pulled a tissue from her pocket to stop the bleeding.

"What happened?" Mrs. Zork asked. "What's that red stuff?"

"My nose is bleeding," Liza told her, and showed her the tissue.

Mrs. Zork jumped back and looked at the blood-splattered table. "Oh my goodness! We must get you to the nurse right away."

The kids watched Mrs. Zork take Liza from the room. "She acted like she'd never seen blood before," Howie whispered.

"At least not red blood," Melody said.

ZING. A gray blob flew past Howie's head and splatted against the concrete wall.

"What was that?" Howie yelped.

"I just made one of your famous flying saucers," Eddie laughed. Then he snatched another glob of clay. "I can make more, too!"

Howie grabbed the clay. "Give me that!"

"This is our chance to have some fun," Eddie said, taking a green paint can off the shelf. "Let's spray paint the windows while Mrs. Zork is gone." Eddie squirted a white blob of paint on the nearest window. "Hey! Somebody switched the labels. This is supposed to be green."

Howie grabbed the can from Eddie. "Quit that, you moron. This is our chance to find out what happened to Mr. Gibson."

"What do you think you'll find?" Eddie laughed. "A tied-up art teacher in the filing cabinet?"

"Of course not," Melody interrupted. "But we might find a clue." With that the three children started peeping in cupboards and boxes. The rest of the third-graders were busy making clay pots.

Melody pointed to Mrs. Zork's open briefcase. "Look at this!"

"It's just an old newspaper," Eddie said.

Melody nodded. "It's a ten-year-old article about an alien space craft."

"Maybe she collects old newspapers to line her bird cage with," Eddie said.

"Then how do you explain this?" Howie asked as he pulled another paper from the briefcase.

"Easy," Eddie said. "It's a map. You can line a bird cage with those, too."

"That's not any map," Melody said. "It's a star map."

Howie nodded. "And somebody's charted a course on it."

"Some kid was probably playing connect-the-dots with the stars," Eddie laughed.

"Maybe," Howie said. "Or maybe somebody was making travel plans."

"That's silly," Melody giggled. "Nobody travels in space."

"Nobody," Howie said slowly, "except aliens."

4

The Surprise of Their Lives

Right after art class, Mrs. Jeepers took the third-graders to recess.

"Phe-ew," Melody said when they walked out the door. "It smells like burnt rubber."

"If you'd take a bath once in a while, maybe it wouldn't stink so bad," Eddie laughed.

"It smells just like my dad's lab coat," Howie said.

"Then maybe he needs a bath, too," Eddie said as he ran to the huge oak tree in the playground. His friends followed him to their usual meeting place.

Eddie hung upside down from a branch and blew spit bubbles. "You're strange, Eddie," Melody told him.

"What's really strange is that art teacher," Howie said.

Eddie jumped down from the tree. "I could've sworn she had dull metal braces when I saw her in the office. But they looked really shiny in art class."

"Maybe she cleaned them," Melody said.

Howie shook his head. "But don't you think it's odd the way she came out of nowhere? And don't forget Mr. Gibson's disappearance!"

"She's just a crazy art teacher. Come on, I'll show you," Eddie bragged as he walked away.

"Where are we going?" Liza squeaked.

"We're going to spy on her. And if you don't come, that means you're a chicken!" Eddie told them.

The four kids sneaked around the building to the art room window. They had to stand on tiptoes to peek inside. Mrs. Zork stood in front of the classroom television.

She was watching Melody's favorite cartoon, *Puddle Blasters*.

"I love this part," Melody whispered. "This is where Puddle Man turns the desert into a huge flower garden."

"Look at all those pretty pink flowers," Liza sighed.

"Mrs. Zork likes them," Howie said as Mrs. Zork reached out and touched the flowers. When she did, her long white hair started to move.

"The static in the TV is making her hair stick straight up," Eddie laughed. "She looks like the Bride of Frankenstein."

"Something's wrong," Liza interrupted. "The flowers are fading." She was right. The bright cartoon petunias were soon black and white.

"The TV must be broken," Melody shrugged.

"I'm not so sure," Howie said slowly. But before they could say more, Mrs.

Zork turned in their direction. A pink streak of light flashed from her braces.

"Let's get out of here!" Howie yelled. The four kids raced around the building. They were panting when they reached the oak tree.

"Why did you run?" Eddie snapped.

Howie faced his friends. "Didn't you see how her braces turned pink?"

Eddie shrugged. "It was just the sun shining on them."

"Then explain why the pink flowers in the cartoon faded."

His three friends laughed at Howie. "Because it's an old TV," Melody told him.

Howie looked at his friends. Then he spoke very slowly. "That old newspaper article and star map reminded me of something I heard my dad talk about with the scientists from the Federal Aeronautics Technology Station."

Eddie laughed. "Those scientists at FATS spend all their time talking about aliens and flying saucers."

"Exactly," Howie whispered. "I think Mrs. Zork is an alien."

His three friends laughed.

"Aliens are little green men with antennas," Eddie snickered.

Melody nodded. "They don't just land their flying saucers on the playground and decide to be art teachers!"

"And they definitely don't wear braces," Liza giggled.

Howie pointed his finger at his friends. "Remember when the lights went on and off this morning?"

"What about it?" Eddie asked.

"That was probably when she landed. This awful smell is from the spaceship's fumes."

"Next you'll tell us Carey is the Star Fleet Commander." Melody giggled so hard she had to sit down on the ground.

"You can laugh if you want," Howie warned his friends. "But I think Bailey Elementary needs to watch out for Mrs. Zork."

5

UFO

Howie waved a newspaper at his three friends. "Look at these headlines. They're all about flying saucers here in Bailey City." It was the next morning, and the four kids were gathered at their usual meeting place. Bright yellow dandelions surrounded the big oak tree. Eddie kicked a yellow dandelion before grabbing the newspaper to glance at the headlines. "UFOs. Ugly Fat Omelets," he laughed. "There's no such thing as flying saucers."

"You may not believe in Unidentified Flying Objects," Howie said slowly, "but my dad has plenty of books that tell all about them."

"People write books about ghosts, too," Eddie said. "And there's no such thing."

"Well, a lot of people around here do

believe in UFOs," Howie pointed out. "As a matter of fact, there was a famous sighting right here in Bailey City, just ten years ago."

"Yeah, by some nearsighted granny who spotted Principal Davis' bald head shining in the sun," Eddie laughed.

"The article I saw in Mrs. Zork's briefcase was from ten years ago," Melody said slowly.

Howie nodded. "That's the case I'm talking about. The scientists at FATS documented the case."

"Did your dad tell you that?" Liza asked.

"I overheard my dad talking on the phone when I was visiting him last weekend," Howie told her. "When I asked him about it, he wouldn't say anything else. I think it might have something to do with Mrs. Zork. If you promise not to tell a soul, I'll tell you what I heard."

Liza and Melody nodded.

"What about you?" Howie asked Eddie. "Do you promise?"

Eddie shrugged. "Who would I tell?"

The four friends huddled under the oak tree. "Ten years ago," Howie began, "an alien spacecraft was sighted near Bailey City. During the following week, all the flowers faded and died."

"You're making this up," Eddie interrupted. "If that was true, Bailey City would be world famous for their museum of little green men."

Howie shook his head. "It's top secret. The government denies it ever happened because it would cause mass hysteria."

Eddie laughed. "Sounds hysterical to me."

Melody nodded. "Everyone knows the flowers died because the Red River dried up. Besides, if the aliens haven't come back for ten years, why would they come now?" she asked.

"That's what my dad was talking about

on the phone. It has something to do with the alignment of the planets," Howie said. "It's exactly the same as ten years ago. I think the aliens have returned to Bailey City, and Mrs. Zork is one of them."

"I think you have wet noodles for brains," Eddie laughed. With that, he ran into school. The other three kids shrugged as they followed him into the building. But they all froze when they saw Mrs. Zork and Mrs. Jeepers talking in the hall.

Mrs. Zork's hair looked more blonde than white, and her cheeks were pink. "What a lovely pin," she said as she touched the brooch Mrs. Jeepers always wore. "It is such a nice shade of green. I wish we had pins this color where I am from."

Mrs. Jeepers stepped away from the new art teacher. "Thank you very much," she said softly. "It is very special."

Mrs. Zork nodded. "It highlights your beautiful red hair."

Mrs. Jeepers glanced at Mrs. Zork, but her eyes didn't flash like they usually did.

The four kids followed Mrs. Jeepers into the classroom. "Did you see Mrs. Zork's hair?" Melody whispered. "It's a different color."

"She probably dyed it," Eddie snapped.

"Well, I think she looks better with makeup," Melody told her friends. "She looked dead yesterday."

Howie nodded. "Mrs. Jeepers sure could use some of that makeup. She looks exhausted."

It was true. Mrs. Jeepers was pale and even her green eyes seemed dull. Her red hair lacked its usual shine and her brooch looked cloudy.

"Maybe she's sick," Eddie whispered. "I bet we can get away with stirring up some trouble."

Then Eddie went into action. While Carey sharpened her pencil, he drew a big red "F" on her homework paper. When Carey saw it she squealed, "Mrs. Jeepers! Eddie drew all over my homework! It's ruined."

The class held their breath as Mrs. Jeepers stood up from her desk. She glared at Eddie and then slowly rubbed her brooch.

Eddie waited for a split second and then grinned. "It's party time," he whispered under his breath. Then he hopped on his seat and did a little jig.

"Are you crazy?" Howie hissed as he pulled Eddie down. "She'll turn you into bat bait!"

Eddie shook his head. "She's lost it. She's lost her power. Just look at her."

All the kids stared at Mrs. Jeepers. They held their breath as she pulled the brooch off her starched white blouse.

When she saw the faded stone, she gasped. Without another word, Mrs. Jeepers rushed from the room.

6

Makeup Crazy

Eddie didn't waste a second. As soon as Mrs. Jeepers left he ransacked her desk for tomorrow's homework answers. He ducked under the desk when Principal Davis popped his bald head in the door. "Students," he announced, "Mrs. Jeepers has taken ill. Line up at the door and I will take you to art."

As the kids followed Principal Davis out the door, Eddie sneaked to the end of the line. "I hope Mrs. Jeepers is going to be okay," Liza whispered to him.

"Mrs. Jeepers has never been okay," Eddie sneered. "I don't know why she would start now."

"I've never seen her act like that," Melody pointed out. "Something was terribly wrong with her brooch."

"It was fading," Howie murmured. The four kids were quiet as Principal Davis looked back at him. As he walked in silence, Howie noticed the artwork in the hall. Brightly colored clown pictures were stapled on a cork strip lining the hallway. Howie looked at each picture. The closer he got to the art room, the more faded the clowns looked.

"Weren't these pictures brighter yesterday?" Howie wondered out loud.

"Shhh." Principal Davis gave him a stern look.

Howie bit his lip and walked quietly into the art room with his friends. When Mrs. Zork smiled at them, her braces glowed pink. Her lips were bright pink and it looked as if she had used a bottle of pink paint on her cheeks. Even her hair had an extra glow to it.

"Mrs. Zork must have started beauty school," Melody giggled under her breath.

"It looks like she drained the color from this room," Howie whispered. Melody, Liza, and Eddie looked around. The blackboard was gray, the construction paper was pale, and even the bottles of paint looked drab.

"It looks like Eddie poured brown paint over everything," Melody whispered.

"Don't look at me," Eddie muttered.

"You're right," Mrs. Zork interrupted. "Right now, you need to look at me. It is time for another pottery lesson. Do we have a volunteer?"

Everyone but Eddie, Melody, Howie, and Liza raised their hands. Mrs. Zork called on Carey. "I just love your bright pink sweatshirt. I wish I had something that color," she said as Carey grabbed a blob of clay. Howie's eyes grew wide as Mrs. Zork lightly touched the arm of Carey's shirt.

"What's the matter?" Eddie asked him.

"Tell you later," Howie said and moved

as far away from Mrs. Zork as he could.

Art class seemed to last forever. Howie had never been so glad to see Principal Davis' shiny head in all his life. "I'm taking you out for an early recess," Principal Davis told the class. He pretended not to notice the scramble behind him as everyone tried to be first in line. Everyone but Howie, that is.

"What's wrong with you?" Melody asked as they gathered under the oak tree. "You look like Superman just spit in your face."

"Didn't you notice anything on the way to the art room?" Howie asked.

"Yeah, I noticed Principal Davis' underwear was sticking out of his pants," Melody said rolling her eyes.

Howie shook his head. "I'm talking about all the pictures. They were faded."

"That's just the sun," Liza piped up. "It

always fades stuff that's hanging."

"Didn't the art room look different to you?" Howie asked.

"It's the same stupid art room," Eddie shrugged. "Only now it's got a makeup-crazy substitute in it."

"I don't think she's makeup crazy," Howie said. "I think she's color crazy."

"Huh?" Melody, Liza, and Eddie said together.

"Don't you remember Mrs. Zork touching Mrs. Jeepers' brooch this morning?" Howie said.

"So? Maybe she likes old jewelry," Melody said.

"Right after that, Mrs. Jeepers starting acting funny and her brooch looked different," Howie reminded them.

"Almost like it was losing its color!" Liza chimed in.

"And look at Carey's shirt." Howie pointed to the swings where Carey played. Her shirt was no longer as pink as bubble gum. Now it was a mucky brown.

"She must've splattered it with that yucky clay," Melody said.

"I don't think so," Howie said slowly. "It's fading just like the flowers faded ten years ago."

"What in the world are you talking about?" Eddie snapped.

"I'm talking about an alien stealing our colors," Howie whispered.

7

Green Cheese
and Laser Guns

"Mrs. Zork is no alien and I can prove it," Eddie bragged.

"How?" Melody asked.

"Simple," Eddie told them. "I'll follow her home."

"What will that prove?" Liza asked.

Eddie kicked at a rock lying on the ground. "Any self-respecting alien is bound to have green cheese or laser guns lying around. I'll peek in her window and see that she's just an ordinary teacher."

"Isn't peeking into somebody's house against the law?" Liza asked.

Eddie shrugged. "I've peeked in plenty of windows before."

"I guess it is the only way to find out about Mrs. Zork," Melody agreed.

"We'll wait until she leaves," Eddie

told them. "Then we'll follow her home."

"I just hope she doesn't leave in a spaceship," Howie muttered.

After school the four kids hid behind the Dumpster. Soon Mrs. Zork rushed out of the school. Her braces sparkled bright pink when she glanced up at the sky.

"I bet she's looking for her spaceship," Howie whispered.

"Did you see her braces?" Liza squealed. "They changed colors again. Maybe she is an alien."

"Her braces probably measure all the color she's stolen," Howie told them.

"Naw. She's just a bad aim with her lipstick," Eddie said.

"Shhh," Melody warned. The four kids waited for Mrs. Zork to walk half a block before they followed cautiously. Mrs. Zork lived on Zender Street in a small white house with black shutters. Behind the tiny house was a gravel driveway

leading to an old rundown garage.

"She isn't an alien any more than you are," Eddie said when he saw Mrs. Zork's house.

"Don't be so sure," Howie told him. "Let's look around back." The four friends sneaked around the side of the house. A huge black satellite dish took up nearly half the backyard.

"There's proof," Howie hissed. "She's probably receiving secret messages from her mother ship in outer space."

Eddie rolled his eyes. "A lot of people have satellite dishes," he snapped. "Maybe Mrs. Zork likes to watch foreign films."

Howie glared at Eddie and then crept up to the garage windows with his three friends close behind. Without a word, they peered inside. What they saw took their breath away.

8

Great Martians Alive

Inside the dingy garage was a white dome that looked like a huge turtle shell. Pale pink and green lights blinked all around its base.

"Gosh!" Liza whispered.

"It can't be real," Melody insisted.

"There's only one way to find out," Eddie said. "I'm going in."

"You can't just walk into an alien's garage," Liza whispered. "You could get arrested for trespassing."

"Who'd arrest me?" Eddie snapped. "The space cadets?" He slowly turned the rusty doorknob. The door creaked open and Eddie slipped inside.

"I'm not going in there," Liza whimpered.

"We can't let him go alone," Howie

told her. He took a deep breath and followed his friend.

Melody started to go, but Liza grabbed her. "Don't leave me by myself!"

Melody pulled her arm away. "I'm not about to stay out here where Mrs. Zork can see us. It's safer inside. Now, come on!"

Eddie and Howie were already checking out the odd dome. A strange humming sound came from inside.

"That's the humming sound we heard at school," Liza gulped. "Just before the electricity went dead."

"It's got to be a spaceship," Howie whispered.

"I'll believe that when I see it zoom through the sky," Eddie told them.

"Maybe you'll believe this." Melody pointed to a color chart hanging on the wall next to a large panel of buttons. The word SPECIMENS was stamped on the top of the chart. The kids stared at the names listed down the side. Mrs. Jeepers' name was written in green, Carey's name in pink, and Eddie's name in red.

"Pink and green," Melody whispered. "Just like the blinking lights on this ship!"

"Why does she have my name in her garage?" Eddie asked.

Melody shrugged. "Maybe she's taking human souvenirs back to colonize new planets."

"But why are the names written in different colors?" Liza asked.

"I know!" Howie swallowed hard. "Every person listed on that chart has a color Mrs. Zork wants. She got the green from Mrs. Jeepers' brooch, and the pink from Carey's sweater! It's obvious she's stealing all our colors."

"Who cares about missing colors?" Eddie asked.

Howie pointed to the chart. "You should. Because I think your red hair is next!"

9

Alien Invasion

"Did you tell your dad?" Melody asked Howie the next morning. "Is he going to help us?"

"My father wouldn't believe me," Howie told his friends. They were standing under the oak tree on the playground. A cold breeze made the white dandelions shiver. "He thinks I'm crazy. He said I may need therapy."

Eddie punched Howie on the arm. "I always knew you needed a shrink."

"This is no laughing matter," Melody interrupted. "Bailey City is being invaded by aliens."

"One goofy art teacher does not make an invasion," Eddie said.

"Then explain these white dandelions,"

Howie said. "And the spaceship in her garage."

"Spaceship?" a soft voice came from behind.

"MRS. ZORK!" Liza squealed. "We didn't see you!"

The four friends faced the new art teacher. She was wearing a bright green jumpsuit with a pink scarf around her waist. A white dandelion was in her yellow hair.

Melody put her hands on her hips. "But we did see a spaceship in your garage."

Mrs. Zork frowned at the four children. Her braces sparked hot pink when she smiled. "You must mean my kiln. I use it for firing pottery."

"If that's a kiln, then I'm a monkey's uncle," Eddie told her.

Mrs. Zork slowly patted Eddie on his head. "Do not be silly. You look nothing like a monkey. Now you children must go to class."

The four kids followed Mrs. Zork into the building. "I told you it wasn't a spaceship," Eddie laughed. "It's just an oven for baking clay!"

"Maybe you're right," Liza said softly.

"Then what's happening to Eddie's hair?" Melody asked.

10

Drained

Eddie rushed to the bathroom to check his hair. "What are you talking about? I've still got my hair," Eddie snapped when he came out. "It's probably bleached from playing in the sun yesterday."

"She did it to you!" Melody said. "She stole your red hair."

"You can think what you want," Howie told Eddie. "But I know Mrs. Zork is stealing all our colors. And if we don't do something about it, we're doomed to live in a gray-and-white world."

Eddie laughed. "Who cares?"

Liza pointed inside their classroom. "You will care if we end up with Principal Davis as our substitute for the rest of the year."

Eddie groaned. Everybody knew that Principal Davis was the toughest teacher to ever hit an elementary school. His idea of fun was copying hundreds of math problems from the board. He was already busy filling up the board with double-digit multiplication problems.

"We haven't even learned that yet," Liza whimpered as they went into their room.

Principal Davis smiled from behind his glasses. "Then it's about time you did. I'm looking forward to teaching it to you today."

"Where's Mrs. Jeepers?" Melody asked. "Is she still sick?"

Principal Davis nodded. "She's feeling a little drained. She won't be back until her color is normal. I couldn't get a substitute teacher. So you're stuck with me. Luckily, we have plenty to keep us busy."

The class had no time to groan before they started copying math problems.

After that they did ten pages from their English book, seven pages from their social studies book, read three chapters from a funny story, and did every magnet experiment from their science book. And that was all before lunch!

By the time they reached the cafeteria, the kids looked as if they had run the Boston Marathon.

"I'm too tired to eat," Melody complained when she sat down with a tray.

"We'd better eat," Liza told them. "We need all our strength for this afternoon!"

"Principal Davis is working our fingers off," Eddie griped as he bit into a hot dog. "There's no telling what he'll make us do after lunch."

"Or tomorrow," Howie added, waving a french fry. "And the day after, and for the rest of the year."

"What do you mean?" Melody asked.

"Mrs. Jeepers is never coming back,"

Howie said slowly. "Not until we get her color back."

Eddie shook his head. "Why should we help? I never liked her anyway."

"We have to help her," Howie said softly. "Unless you want to be stuck with Principal Davis for the rest of the year."

Eddie swallowed hard and nodded. His voice was hoarse when he said, "We'll meet under the oak tree when it gets dark."

11

"We Know Who You Are"

Howie stood under the oak tree and checked his neon-orange glow-in-the-dark watch. The night air sent chills up his back, and the crooked branches of the oak tree made an eerie pattern against the starry sky. Finally, Eddie came jogging up the street.

"Where have you been?" Howie shivered and pulled his jacket tight.

"I had to wait for Dad to fall asleep," he answered. "Where are Liza and Melody?"

"I guess they couldn't make it," Howie said. "C'mon. Let's head for Mrs. Zork's place."

The two boys headed down Zender Street, making sure to stay in the shadows. The street was still and quiet. Many of the houses were brightly lit. The blue glow of TVs came from many of them, but Mrs. Zork's house was totally dark.

"Maybe nobody's home," Eddie whispered. "Let's go check out the garage." The two boys shivered in the night wind as they crept around back.

A low humming sound came from the strange object, and the blinking lights made eerie shadows on the wall. Howie pointed to the new row of red lights.

"There's the red from your hair. We have to get the colors out."

The two boys searched for an entrance to the object. "There's no opening," Howie said.

Eddie pointed to the panel of buttons on the side. "Maybe one of these will get it open." Then he started punching the buttons.

"Don't push those," Howie squeaked. "You don't know what you're doing."

It was too late. The top of the dome lifted up. But before they had a chance to look inside, they heard a soft voice behind them.

"What are you boys doing in my garage?" said a voice so quiet that Eddie could barely make out the words.

"We've come to save our colors," Howie said bravely.

Mrs. Zork laughed and her braces sparked in the dim light of the dome.

"We know who you are," Howie said, "and why you're here. We won't let you get away with it."

Mrs. Zork put a long skinny hand on Howie's neon-orange glow-in-the-dark watch. "Eddie, help me," Howie squeaked.

Eddie put his hand on a large black switch. "Let go of him, or I'll send your spaceship back into orbit."

"What?" Mrs. Zork said, holding fast to Howie.

"Maybe this will get your attention!" Eddie hollered and flipped the switch. A loud *ping* rang throughout the garage and the lights flickered.

"Stop that at once," Mrs. Zork demanded.

Eddie placed a finger on the blinking red button. "Not until you let Howie go."

Mrs. Zork's hand slipped away and

Howie quickly moved beside Eddie. "Make her let the colors out, too," Howie told Eddie.

"You heard him," Eddie said to Mrs. Zork. "Let them go. You have until the count of five, then I'm going to push this button."

"Stay away. Its very hot!" Mrs. Zork's braces sparked more than usual in the dark garage.

"One, two, three, four. . . ." Eddie counted. "Only one more and then your precious spaceship is spare parts."

Mrs. Zork's braces were a bright glowing red when Eddie hollered, "FIVE!" He leaned with all his might on the red button.

Red coils lit up and steam came from the bottom of the dome. The entire garage started shaking and a high-pitched squealing filled the air.

"That thing's going to explode!" Eddie screeched.

Howie grabbed Eddie's arm. "Let's get out of here before this whole garage blows up."

At the end of Zender Street they stopped to catch their breath. Over Mrs. Zork's house, a fountain of sparks arched high in the air like a burning rainbow.

12

Flu Season?

Melody was under the big oak tree the next morning picking a bright yellow dandelion when Howie and Eddie got there. "What happened at Mrs. Zork's last night?" she asked.

Howie looked at Eddie. They hadn't figured out what to tell their friends. Luckily, Liza skipped up to the tree and changed the subject. "Did you guys see those strange streaks of light in the sky last night?" she asked.

"It was probably the auto dealer having a sale," Melody said. "They always shine these big spotlights up in the sky. Once I thought one was a UFO!"

"It looked more like fireworks to me," Liza said. Then she looked at Eddie. "Your hair's bright red again!"

Eddie shrugged. "It's the same hair. It must be the way the sun is shining on it. I'm surprised it's not gray from all the work Principal Davis made us do yesterday."

"There's no telling what he has in store for us today," Melody groaned. "I guess we better head inside and find out."

Howie and Eddie were quiet as they walked into the classroom. They didn't know what to do about Mrs. Zork, but they both forgot all about her when they saw Mrs. Jeepers was back.

"Good morning, students," she said in her strange accent. She was wearing a crisp white blouse, and at her throat sparkled the bright green brooch.

"Were you sick?" Carey asked.

Mrs. Jeepers' eyes flashed, but then she smiled. "I was a little peaked, but I feel much better now. Unfortunately, I have some bad news. There was an explosion in Mrs. Zork's garage last night. It seems that her kiln went up in smoke."

"It went up all right," Eddie mumbled.

"Did you say something, Eddie?" Mrs. Jeepers asked as she touched her brooch.

"Uh . . . I said . . . is Mrs. Zork all right?" Eddie stammered.

Mrs. Jeepers smiled. "Luckily, no one was injured. However, Principal Davis was notified that there was quite a bit of damage done to her home, so she must move."

"Do you mean Mrs. Zork won't be coming back to Bailey Elementary?" Liza asked.

"I am afraid not," Mrs. Jeepers said. "But the good news is that Mr. Gibson is back with us after his bout with the flu. He was so ill, he slept through most of this week."

As the kids walked to art, they noticed new colorful pictures hanging on the walls. Even the pictures by the art room were bright and cheerful.

"We helped after all," Howie whispered to Eddie. "You must have released the colors when you pushed the red button."

"This is one time I'm glad everything is back to normal," Eddie said.

"Me, too," Liza sighed.

Melody nodded. "But things never stay normal for long at Bailey Elementary!"

Debbie Dadey and Marcia Thornton Jones have fun writing stories together. When they both worked at an elementary school in Lexington, Kentucky, Debbie was the school librarian and Marcia was a teacher. During their lunch break in the school cafeteria, they came up with the idea of the Bailey School kids.

Recently Debbie and her family moved to Plano, Texas. Marcia and her husband still live in Kentucky where she continues to teach. How do these authors still write together? They talk on the phone and use computers and fax machines!